DIRTY SEX STORIES

EXPLICIT DIRTY EROTICA SHORT STORIES

SHON GACY, JULLES MUNSEN, SAGE
YARBER,ARIELLE FOSSETT, PORTIS
NEWMAN,EFRAIN MALLERY,NICHOLE
ROGUE, GARRETT ZEIGER,SHALA BREECE

plicit Press

CHAPTER 1

LOVE IS IN THE AIR

THE HAND that slid around Kaylea Daniels's waist left an electric trail across her skin. The twenty-two-year-old looked over her shoulder in the mirror. A pair of powder blue eyes peered back at her, the lust in them making her pussy wet.

"Think your cousin will notice if we don't show up?" Twenty-four-year-old Orrin Barker spread his hand across Kaylea's stomach. He nuzzled aside her chestnut brown hair and pressed his lips against the hollow under her ear.

"Considering I'm a bridesmaid, I think she might," Kaylea's dark gray eyes traced over Orrin's familiar face. Thick sienna hair that needed a trim. Strong jaw. A nose that might've been a bit too long.

"Too bad," Orrin slid his hand up to cover her breast, long fingers over black lace until the tips brushed the top of her creamy flesh. His other hand caressed her hip before running over the matching black panties to cup her sex. "I really wanted to take these off." One finger pressed against the damp crotch of her underwear.

"Mmm," Kaylea moaned, pushing her ass back against Orrin's erection.

"But," Orrin removed his hands and took a step back, earning a dirty look from Kaylea. "If you're sure, we'd better go."

Kaylea stood in line with the rest of the bridal party, decidedly uncomfortable in the floor-length magenta gown. Her eyes kept returning to her boyfriend, finding him easily, feeling his eyes on her.

He'd smiled during the ceremony. Watched her as he left the receiving line. Watched her eat. And now, as the bride and groom had their first dance, she knew his gaze was on her again. She shifted, thighs rubbing together. She'd been horny since Orrin's little pre-wedding visit and it had just gotten worse as the night wore on.

The second the groomsman released her hands, Kaylea found herself in Orrin's arms. She sighed, a sense of relief washing over her. The ache between her legs was still there, but the tension had melted into a smolder.

"Come with me," Kaylea took Orrin's hand and pulled him off the dance floor. "Kaylea?" Her name was a question, not a protest.

Kaylea had spotted the door earlier that night and had made a mental note of it. Now, she led Orrin into the supply closet, using the glimpse of light before the door closed to find the light switch. She spun around and shoved Orrin back against the door, plastering herself to his body before he could speak. Her mouth covered his, lips forcing hers apart.

If Orrin was surprised by Kaylea's ferocity, he didn't let it faze him. His hands slid over her hips and then further down to cup her ass. His tongue tangled with hers as she buried her hands in his hair.

Kaylea writhed against her boyfriend, the hard planes of his body responding to hers. He always responded to her. They'd known each other since childhood and had been together four years, moving to Charleston after he'd graduated from college. And still, they never tired of each other.

She shoved her hand down the front of his suit pants, eliciting a gasp that she quickly swallowed. As she worked open his pants and grasped his hard cock, Orrin was pulling up her skirt. She stroked him once, twice, her grip just this side of painful.

Orrin hooked her knee over his arm, teeth scraping over her bottom lip. Kaylea moaned into his mouth as she reached between them to yank the crotch of her panties to one side. She pulled away from his mouth and locked her eyes with his.

"Kay," Orrin ground out as he buried himself in her wet heat.

Kaylea cried out as her boyfriend's impressive girth forced its way inside. The sensation of being stretched, of being filled, the hours of waiting... she was cumming even before he was done moving. Her body was still shaking when Orrin began to thrust up into her, the force of each stroke lifting her off her foot.

She dropped her head to his shoulder, letting the pleasure take over. Orrin was her perfect fit, the one who could play her body like a fine instrument. It didn't matter if he was taking his time, hours of his mouth on her pussy, driving her over the edge into seemingly endless bliss, or if it was hard and fast like this.

A whimper escaped Kaylea's lips as another orgasm rocked through her. She could feel her muscles trembling and knew if she came again, she would probably pass out. When things were this intense with Orrin, when he was so far inside her that she believed they could merge into a single organism, she could never tell how her body was going to react. She mouthed at Orrin's neck, worrying at the skin with teeth and lips.

"Mark me," Orrin whispered. "Mark me so that when we go back out there, everyone knows that I belong to someone. That I belong to you."

His words sent a shiver down her spine and she sucked skin into her mouth, drawing blood to the surface.

"That's it," Orrin grunted as his hips jerked. "Now, cum again." Kaylea made an inarticulate noise, but Orrin knew what she meant.

"It's okay, lover," Orrin spoke through gritted teeth, fighting his body's natural instinct to just let go. "I've got you."

His word, the truth behind them, was the mental nudge to push her body over the physical edge. Kaylea cried out his name, leg buckling, arms clinging to his neck. The change in weight drove Orrin deeper and he exploded inside her. Everything went white as Kaylea felt the familiar sensation of Orrin's cock pulsing, emptying inside her.

Her eyes fluttered open to see Orrin grinning down at her. They were sitting on the floor and she was cradled in his lap.

"Feel better?" Orrin's eyes sparkled.

. . .

"Much," Kaylea returned his smile. As she stood, however, she frowned. Her eyes met Orrin's. He read the question on her face and answered it. "I told you I wanted to take them off of you."

He held up a hand, Kaylea's panties handing from one finger.

"Orrin," Kaylea made to grab the garment but Orrin yanked back his hand, shoving the panties into his suit pocket as he stood. "You can't expect me to go out there without..."

"I can," Orrin's smile widened. "And you will." His voice lowered into the familiar authoritative tone Kaylea knew well.

Things low in her belly tightened, her cheeks flushing as she became aware of Orrin's seed trickling down the inside of her leg. She was going to do it. She was going to walk back into the wedding sans underwear.

And she was going to love every second of it.

CHAPTER 2

CARNAL FANTASIES

"DON'T EVER LEAVE ME, CARL," she'd told him, as he cuddled her in his strong muscular arms. It had been a while since she'd felt the soft tender touch of her husband Carl. He was always terribly busy at the office and when he came home, he was always too tired to do anything, or she was too tired to even roll over to kiss him goodnight.

However last night had been different. He'd come to her and pleased her like he'd never done before. His kisses on her skin had as gentle as ever, while he whispered sweet nothings into her ear. Sandy hadn't been sure whether she'd been dreaming or not. This was totally unlike her husband.

Carl Armstrong had been her husband and the love of her life. They'd met in high school and developed a close friend-ship from there. When she went to NYU, he followed her there, saying that he didn't want her in a different state from where he was. After college, they both got good jobs and worked hard. When they finally got married, he promised her that he would never leave her, or hurt her. Had he forgotten his little promise to her?

During recent times, her husband had had several mistresses. Some of which made no effort to conceal that they were sleeping with him. It was almost as if some of them were gloating to her. She'd felt used and embarrassed, until last night. Last night was different, so different that it almost felt like there was a stranger in her bed. Was this her Carl? Could he have changed so much? Sandy hadn't told him anything for fear that it might disrupt their romantic evening. But now, in the morning, she couldn't help but realize that she was experiencing one of two things, she was either reliving a memory or fantasizing about being with her husband. How he made time for his mistresses and never made time for her, she never understood.

Sandy woke up to once again find herself alone, but this time she relaxed and allowed herself time to revel in the outcome of yesterday. The bed was a messy reminder of the activity between her and Carl last night, which brought a smile to her face. She rolled onto her back and stretched out her arms and legs, with nothing short of a big grin on her face. She was sure that there were many women who would not even contemplate the idea of having sex with two men in one day; in fact, a week ago she would have been one of those women! Yet her memories of yesterday were arousing and invigorating.

. . .

She let her hand slowly caress her own body as she kicked the sheets back and recalled the excitement that yesterday had held. Even though her commitment to her husband was once again strong and true, she could not help but close her eyes and imagine the strong, youthful body of David hovering over her. The way he had made her feel as he had pleasured her with his tongue, his lips, and his mouth, all on top of her, and between her legs and within her, making her whole pussy throb and resonate in a way she had never even thought possible.

As she lay there, spread out on the bed, she let her hand absent-mindedly slip between her thighs and her fingers seek out her clitoris and gently massage in gentle, indecisive circles. She recalled how he'd taken her under the waterfall, with no holding back. She couldn't help but smirk at herself at the thought of taking a man, so much her junior, in such a wanton way. After so many years of marriage, she had never imagined the possibility of corrupting such a young man. Or had he corrupted her?

Her hand started to move with more urgency as she thought about even the possibility of attracting a man so much younger than herself, and she gave out a little groan as she thought about how he'd taken her so completely as the sound of the water crashing down had filled her ears so that all her senses we heightened and taking in every last drop of the surroundings. Then she had returned home only to find Carl hungry for her, despite his upset and anger he had been able to hide his longing for her in his eyes. She bore her hips down into the mattress, and slowly rotated them in the opposite direction with her fingers. Her groaning was no longer concealed as she grew wetter; she brought her fingers to her mouth and licked off her fingertips, tasting her own erotic juices.

What did these men taste in her? What was so special about her body? She was feeling hot now, no longer concentrating on what had happened the day before, but more concerned about letting herself enjoy the moment now.

She rolled over and came up on her hands and knees like a dog, she took one of the many pillows on the bed a placed it by her slit, letting her juices spill onto it as she rocked herself gently back and forth, rubbing her clitoris on it is a way she could never do with her hand alone. Her orgasm rose in her quicker than she expected, and shuddered through her whole body with exquisite waves of warm pleasure. When she was complete, she rolled back onto her back and stretched out, filling the bed as much as a person of her size could.

Whoever thought she needed a man to complete her was terribly wrong, she'd just peaked her earth-shattering climax all on her own, Sandy thought to herself, looking at the ceiling in the process. The sound of the key rattling outside of the door let her know that she about to have company. She quickly scurried into her clothes, hoping that she would not get caught by whoever was about to enter the room.

CHAPTER 3

COOKING LONG BONELESS GUMBO

HEATHER WALKED LIKE A STRIPPER, talked like a stripper, and when I served her chicken gumbo soup for lunch, discovered she was an ex-stripper. She dressed like a business-woman in a white A-lined skirt, red button blouse, and low-heeled red pumps. On the restaurant table, an attaché case opened with some marketing paper spread out over the top.

A little chicken gumbo spilled on my hands, so I wiped my white apron to keep them from being sticky.

"Hope you enjoy your meal," I said being extra courteous. Lunch was a slow time in our schedule so I could take the time. Several empty white-cloth tables kept the two of us company. My assistant, Janey, went to the bank to cash her check. I didn't expect her back for at least thirty minutes.

"And I wish you a pleasant meal too," she said, stirring her spoon into the soup admiring the steam flowing from the bowl.

"Business is slow right now, but when everyone from the tire plant gets off work, I'll be swamped."

She batted her thick-mascaraed eyelids and her pretty blue eyes locked on to my eyes. "Every man has got to eat to keep up his strength."

She dropped her napkin.

I did not think much of it. I bent down to retrieve it for her and she spread her legs. The long leggy blonde-haired woman didn't bother to wear underwear beneath her white A-line skirt. Her earthy scintillating pussy scent remained embedded in my animal brain. Her physical presence made my dick scramble for release and movement. I grabbed another napkin from an adjoining table and placed it by her glass of water.

"I'm a vegetarian," I said in a cool tone determined to return to work in the kitchen.

"I was too, until recently," her eyes fixed on the growing crotch of my pants, "When I discovered long boneless Gumbo."

"I'm always looking to improve my meal schedule, long boneless Gumbo?"

Heather stood up. "Don't get me all confused in your fantasies. Just because I look like a stripper and talk like a stripper doesn't mean I lost my sexual desire."

While I tried to untangle her sexual innuendo, she grasped my hand and led me around the cashier counter and into my kitchen.

Heather looked around the kitchen and I waited for her to go to the refrigerator, pull out some chicken and demonstrate.

I was surprised again when she squatted, sending her white skirt rising to her twenty-four-inch waist, her bare pussy's thick clit protruding as if to see where the scent of a male came from. By this time, she had my long boneless Gumbo out and was licking my dripping cockhead. She giggled. "Long boneless Gumbo is an old favorite among strippers, wives, and girlfriends."

"Heather . . ." I really must get back to work. "If you are auditioning for a first date..."

Her pink wet tongue darted from her mouth, lathering up the side of my thick hard cock. My cock responded by nuzzling her red-coated lips. Heather took the hint and opened her mouth wide. I slipped down into her wet slobbering mouth. I don't know where my mind went, but my ball sac got hot and started tightening up on my groin, trying to rise out of her seductive hands.

. . .

"Mmmmm," Heather responded. "Mmm-hmmmm."

I interpreted that to mean she accepted my offer for a first date; although in the back of my mind we were heading around third and coming into the home.

"I'm going to blow my jism down your throat—Heather."

I tentatively grabbed her long curly blonde hair. I didn't need to fall down on top of the gorgeous woman I'd just met.

Heather started bobbing her head back and forth on my cock. Soon my dick meat forgot all about the busy schedule three hours away and dove further down her silky throat. My nose didn't want to be left out and sniffed up the musky scent wafting from Heather's spread-legged squat. The sounds of cars in the street disappeared. Sounds I used to let me know when customers arrived or when Janey returned from her lunch break. To my ears, only the sound of Heather's slobbering blowjob on my straining cock mattered. Only the mushy, sticky, squishing loud sounds of Heather's well-oiled girly goo beginning to flow down her legs entranced my ears.

I gave in.

. . .

I grabbed Heather's curly blonde hair by her darkened roots and moved her face and mouth back and forth fast over my long boneless Gumbo dick. I fed her the hottest saltiest meal she desired. I stiffened. My head shot back. I groaned aloud and my first shot of jizz hit her agile pink tongue. Not to be undone, another platoon of my sperm followed the first group man goo flowing down Heather's gullet.

Heather held on tight to my jumping fuck sausage. She drained the small final spurts of my erotic enthusiasm and stood up.

"Relaxed now?" Heather gently grabbed my arms and turned me around as she hopped up on the preparation food table.

"Much better," I had to admit.

She spread her legs. "Now is when you add, some clam meat to that long boneless Gumbo."

She laid back, her white skirt still on her tiny waist. She unbuttoned her red top. She stroked and pulled on her B cup tits. She proudly made love to them so much that I grew to like them as much as she did. And honestly, I'm only a big tit man!

I reached for her hot pink nipples. I leaned forward to lick them. My tongue tasted a hint of sweat and a sweet smell of peaches on her skin. Heather raised her legs. Her knees pinned against my ears as I sucked on her tits. She positioned her bare feet on my hips and pressed back, forcing me to see the wet juncture between her legs.

Her clam salad smelled good. I dove in headfirst. My tongue licked her protruding inner labia lips. Her cunt juices flowed out. Her clit was huge and thick like a piece of rolled chicken. I sucked her clit between my lips and held them while sucking up. Heather squealed and I pressed my hand to silence her. She locked her legs about my upper chest and humped against my face until after a few minutes she went stiff. Her legs held tight. Her sighing moan rang throughout the kitchen as she collapsed into her orgasms.

Janey came through the kitchen door. "Oops!" I pulled back and stared in disbelief.

"Your employees are very loyal," Heather said, lowering her white skirt, slipping on her low-heeled red pumps, and leaving.

"Hi Janey, we—we were discussing a new meal addition." I turned to Heather as she walked pass Janey leaving.

"I'll add that long boneless Gumbo to the special menu. Come back anytime to sample it." "I'll do that," said Heather and I heard her leaving out the door, as the tiny bell rang indicating we had a customer. Heather never did come back, but now Janey wanted some Long Boneless Gumbo. However, that is another story all together.

CHAPTER 4

FUCK MY DUCKY... (NO LAUGHING MATTER)

THE SOUND IS UNMISTAKABLE. Low grunts, the occasional moan, then deep, rapid breathing in vain attempts to stifle sounds. Shanna looks around the corner carefully and spots nothing other than a duck pulling on its own fucking huge, throbbing hard cock. But ducks didn't have cocks, or so her biology teacher had told her in elementary school. Well, at least they didn't have twelve-inch boners that looked like they could turn even the most experienced cunts into duck soup.

The heat under the suit's helmet, a perfect replica of Donald Duck, must be unbearable because without removing the hand dancing rapidly up and down his cock, the man in the chicken suit removes his headdress. He hasn't seen her, hasn't even turned around to see if anyone might have caught his mid-morning masturbation. Nobody ever came down to the service bathroom, *ever*. And he's been working here long enough for forever to be quite a long time. But today Shanna is down here, needing a cigarette without wanting the crowd that gathers for periodic smokes in the back alley of the restaurant. She isn't sure whether to light up or not, not wanting to disturb the company mascot, clearly on his own *smoke* break.

Shanna isn't unattractive. In fact, she's very attractive once you get past her deliberate attempts to mask this. So she's always managed to get fucked, whenever she felt so inclined. This wasn't often, and so the sight of a ready-to-go cock sends immediate I-want-I-want-I-want signals to the depths of her pussy, which responds immediately by wetting itself from the inside. Her smokes and lighter drop to the floor and her hand is immediately under her skirt. Donald Duck turns in horror, caught with his cock in one hand and his beak in the other. His hand keeps moving up and down on his cock despite the flash warnings to abort that is going off in his head. Shanna smiles her most provocative smile and lets her hand disappear even further up her skirt.

Lou, the duck, is on her immediately, locking the door behind them. No words, he's on his knees pulling her panties down. She steps out of the dark lace and then parts her legs so that Lou's head is between them, covered to his shoulders in her striped skirt. She anticipates the heat of his tongue but instead gets sharp cooling streams of air blown directly onto her cunt and then over her inner thigh. This is unexpected and she stumbles. Lou has her legs in his large hands quickly and she steadies herself. The blowing ceases and then the gentlest lips are on her clit. What follows quickly is the most sensuous sucking on her swollen pink lips and then into her vagina.

Lou French kisses her pussy as though they had all the time in the world. The trickle of pussy cum into his mouth reminds him that maybe they don't.

The gentle kissing becomes not-so-gentle fingering as Lou slides two fingers onto her pussy. He does this while getting himself to his feet and finding her mouth. He pushes her against the wall and digs deep into her pussy with his fingers, adding another as his own arousal peaks. His kisses are as passionate as his fingering, rough, rigorous, and determined. Shanna parts her legs both to steady herself and also to allow deeper access. She is practically on her toes now, desperate for his cock inside her so that they can shoot, and get back to work. The tension of being gone too long only fuels the moment and both of them are lost completely to lust.

Lou's digging is so deep and complete that on each dig he lifts Shanna almost completely off the ground. She can't stifle the sounds escaping her mouth. She doesn't want to. He doesn't want her to. Over and over again he sends three fingers in a perfect hook deep into her cunt, each time rendering her airborne. She can only hold onto his broad shoulders for support and hope silently that the next time she lifts off the ground it will be because of his cock. She remembers the long thick veiny tool she had watched him stroke. The huge head would itself be sufficient to work her cunt over completely. She looks down for it, and to her delight, it is as hard and ready as when she first saw it. If she could reach it with her hands she would put it inside her herself. But she has no control over herself with the fingers in her pussy becoming more and more like a seesaw.

Finally her cunt is free, but only briefly. She feels the wet fingers in hers as Lou takes her hands in his and lifts them up over her head. He pins them to the wall behind her. Without using any support he moves his cock into position. The total erection means that he can aim the tool with relative accuracy to wherever he wanted it to be. It isn't hard for him to find the entrance to her cunt. Once on it, he sends his cock into her without too much hesitation, filling her pussy completely. He pushes up hard, going so deep that she lifts off the ground completely again. He pushes up and then forward, pinning her ass to the wall. She struggles briefly but manages to get her legs around his waist. His hands free hers and take a firm grip on her hips. She wraps her hands around his neck, settling her fingers in his hair. Bending his knees slowly he frees some cock while holding Shanna in place. Then he drops her onto his cock, straightening his legs so that again he is in the deepest parts of her vagina.

Shanna squeezes herself tightly onto Lou, pushing her pussy against the cock inside her, intensifying its presence within. Lou's cock is most pleased with her efforts and he multiplies his thrust efforts. He lowers himself further, pushing harder against her so that she is stuck to the wall, and then instead of dropping her onto his cock, he shoots his cock back into her, high, hard, deep. Over and over his cock hits her depths; each stroke ending in a strange quack as he jokingly assumes his character. To add to the joke he turns in the direction of his costume and lifts the head off the floor, putting it on. Pinning her back against the wall Shanna is now face to face with a large, over-animated duckbill. She can't help but giggle, even though the assault on her cunt is anything but a laughing matter.

The head is so huge that it pushes against Shanna's face, knocking her into the wall. If they're to finish up before somebody comes looking for them *or before Shanna has a concussion*, there needs to be a change in position. Lou seems determined to hold on to his head. Thanks to his rigorous gym routine he manages to get down on his haunches, Shanna on his lap, his cock safe inside her. The drop to the floor is swift, the thud excusable. Lou arches back so that his massive head is high enough away from Shanna so that she can relax into the cock ramming into her.

Even the concrete floor isn't cold, just an erotic emphasizing chill. The chill sends shivers through her body and contracts her cunt so that the only response that can come from Lou is an intense downward thrust.

The quacking coming from under the hot head above her has Shanna giggling almost as uncontrollably as her clit is beating just above where twelve inches of Puerto Rican cock is nailing her to the floor. Shanna has no help keeping her legs up since Lou needs to use both his hands to keep himself up, his head weighing him forward. The last thing he needs is to have the massive cranium fall onto Shanna. This would end his delicious exploration into her soft spot almost immediately for sure. His cock would never forgive him. So he plants his hands on either side of her midriff and arches further back so that the head on his shoulders hangs away from her. This has the added benefit of forcing his cock deeper into her.

Shanna places both her feet on the concrete. She has her knees raised so high that her thigh rubs against Lou's forearms. Lou's cock moves deep into her and then out. Inside her, it fills her in every direction. The fat fuck-stick grazes every square inch of her. As he drags it out of her it manages to massage every ripple, every fold of her cunt so that it feels as though he might just turn her pussy inside out. This is suddenly a most delicious prospect along with her orgasm and so she takes both her knees in hand and lifts her feet off the floor. This lift tightens her already tight pussy significantly. Lou's cock is caught in a juicy squeeze that has him move his hands one at a time so that they are placed under her legs, giving them the ability to push Shana's legs as far down as they will go. Her hands are free now and she uses them to pull on her breasts which have been craving attention for some time now.

Finally, Lou can't take it anymore, needing to finish this before he loses his job. Also, his cock is bordering on bruised for all the incessant fucking he's been doing. He sends his cock into her full force and lifts the duck off his head at the same time. He takes less than a second to throw the billed head aside and have his hands back on the ground. With his head free and the renewed ability to breathe, he can focus all his energy now on fucking. This renewed vigor is felt immediately by Shanna and her vagina. With all the power in his ass, he sends his cock deep into her repeatedly. He rams her hard, over and over again, stirring his cock into her depths completely. They are both on the brink of a massive explosion, but Lou knows that Shanna's has to come first. So he keeps pounding her vagina with this thought uppermost in his mind.

He has to lean over her and place his hands on her mouth as she starts to scream profanities, his cock bringing her to a super orgasm. She jerks and writhes under him as he continues thrusting into her. She sends her legs almost straight up into the air, out to the side, and then over his lower back as his cock settles deep inside her again and again. Shanna exhales through her nose, her mouth still covered. She goes still, Lou pausing briefly to allow the winding down of her climax. Then it's his turn, thrusting faster and faster until he is so close to cumming he might not be able to stop himself. He pulls his cock from her with strokes to spare and takes his cock in hand. He is seconds from blowing and his eyes dart around for an ideal target for his load. Suddenly Shanna has her mouth on his cock and moments later her mouth fills with the warmth flowing from Lou. They're both back at work just as soon as they've gathered themselves and shared a cigarette.

CHAPTER 5

SLEEPING WITH THE ENEMY

CAREN DIDN'T KNOW who killed her brother Jerry, but she was willing to find out by any means necessary. For two weeks now, she'd been secretly investigating Marcus Scurfy, the man she believed was responsible for Jerry's murder. If Marcus didn't do it, he must have known who did, she thought. When he'd called her into his office today, she knew that she'd have to do much more than talk to get the answers to her question. But before she got the opportunity to ask him anything, he has some demands of his own.

"I want to fuck you here, in my office, Caren. You've been secretly snooping around my office and I think you need to be taught a lesson." Marcus's voice was low and seductive, and as always, tinged with a hint of something dark. Caren knew he'd never hurt her, but the dark undercurrent to his voice made her insides turn to jelly. How did he know that she had been snooping around his office? He was proving to be much more of a challenge than she'd originally thought.

Marcus reached down and quickly undid the snap and zipper on Caren's jeans, stripping them down her legs. She kicked them away. She was left standing in her bra and panties, while Marcus was still almost completely dressed. She felt somehow exposed and vulnerable, standing in front of the open office windows. She knew Marcus didn't care if someone saw them, but she had the urge to pull him to the floor, out of the line of sight of anyone walking by on the sidewalk. It occurred to her she should get some curtains in here.

Before she could pull Marcus to the floor, he spun her around and pressed his cock against her ass, rubbing it against her panties. He reached up and undid the clasp on her bra, sliding it down her arms, the bra falling to the floor. She gasped at the force of his movement. As she was gaining her balance, Marcus bent her over the desk, reaching around her to sweep a pile of papers aside. He ran his hand over her ass, sliding his fingers beneath the elastic of her panties, his fingers finding their way to her wet and swollen pussy. Caren moaned softly as he slid one finger slowly into her, feeling his cock pressing against her ass.

"You're already wet for me, aren't you, Caren? I like that you're prepared." He pulled his hand away. "I think I can find something more appropriate for that pussy than my finger. Would you like something else in your pussy, Caren? Would you like my cock in your pussy?"

She felt Marcus move away from her briefly and then suddenly her panties were ripped away from her body. She gasped at the sudden tearing sound. Marcus slapped her ass with his hand, making her jump. She yelped in surprise and pleasure.

"So, that excites you. Good. This should too." She felt Marcus's cock rubbing against her hot slit and suddenly, with one thrust, he was inside her, filling her completely. She cried out as he thrust into her again, hard. She braced herself against the desk as Marcus started pounding into her, thrusting himself completely into Caren with each stroke, almost knocking the breath from her.

He held her hips, pulling her back against him with each stroke. Caren spread her legs for balance and bent further over the desk, giving him more access. She heard him grunt and felt him thrust even deeper into her pussy. She snaked one hand down between her legs, finding her hard and swollen clit and began rubbing herself with her fingers.

Marcus picked up the pace, leaning over her, pinning her to the desk. He reached around and grabbed a breast, his hand convulsively crushing it in time with his thrusts. Caren could feel he was intent on making this a quick session; his thrusts took on a frantic pace, and his rhythm became the slightest bit unsteady. She was very close herself, her fingers rapidly working her clit.

She felt herself coming then, her stomach muscles contracting, bending her knees as she climaxed. She cried out as a wave of pleasure broke over her. She felt Marcus's breath hot on her neck and heard the small grunting noise he made with each stroke that meant he was very close. She turned her head slightly.

"Come on, baby, come for me. Fill me up." She barely breathed the words before Marcus cried out, his cock suddenly exploding inside her, hot liquid filling her pussy. She cried out again her own second wave of orgasm flooded through her, as both of them sought their release.

Marcus lay panting on top of her, his cock still twitching inside her pussy, holding her against his body. He was covered with a sheen of sweat; she could feel the trickles running down her back, feel the heat between them.

Marcus finally pulled her down on the thick rug,

pillowing her head on his chest, and wrapping his arms around her. Amazingly they drifted off, both sated, the sun through the uncontained windows making them drowsy.

The buzzing of the phone brought them awake. Marcus sat up, fishing around on the desk until he located the phone.

"Shutter here," he barked. "Oh, Jeffrey, hi. Didn't see the caller ID, sorry." Caren watched Marcus listening intently, and then his face broke into a wide grin. "Great! Thanks. I told you they'd go for it. Okay. Make the arrangements and we'll meet you at the airport in a couple hours." Marcus tossed the phone back on his desk.

He settled back on the floor, looking very pleased with himself. Caren had no idea what he was talking about.

"Good news I presume," Caren sat up, looking under the desk for her bra and sweater. She retrieved her clothes, and then remembered her panties were a casualty of Marcus's aggressive hands.

Marcus rolled on his side, leaning on his elbow. "I just bought a new company." His voice was low.

Caren looked at Marcus. " You did?"

"Yes I surely did," Marcus looked at her closely. "Are you surprised?"

Marcus got up to leave, just then Caren held his hand. "I need to ask you something. It's about my brother." His look immediately darkened, and Caren felt it - he knew exactly what happened to her brother.

ABOUT THE AUTHOR

Arielle Fossett is an emerging erotica author of many erotica kinks and sub-genres. Be sure to check out other books and leave a review if this story got you hot!

Visit my blog at Arielle Fossett's Blog

Join my newsletter for the exclusiveArielle Fossett's Newsletter

Sign up for Free Stories from Xplicit Press Authors

Xplicit Press Author Updates

Like Xplicit Press on Facebook

Follow Xplicit Press on Twitter

Readers: I want to expand a few of the stories to see where the characters can be explored further. If there are any of the stories that you would like to read more about again, I'd love to hear from you!

Keep In Touch
Arielle Fossett
info@ariellefossett.com